Ride a Cock-Horse

Chosen by Sarah Williams
Illustrated by Ian Beck

D1308804

Oxford University Press

Oxford University Press, Walton Street, Oxford OX2 6DP

Oxford New York
Athens Auckland Bangkok Bombay
Calcutta Cape Town Dar es Salaam Delhi
Florence Hong Kong Istanbul Karachi
Kuala Lumpur Madras Madrid Melbourne
Mexico City Nairobi Paris Singapore
Taipei Tokyo Toronto

and associated companies in
Berlin Ibadan

Oxford is a trade mark of Oxford University Press

Illustrations © Ian Beck 1986
Selection, arrangement and editorial matter
© Oxford University Press 1986
First published 1986
Reprinted 1988 (twice)
First published in paperback 1988
Reprinted 1988 (twice), 1990, 1991, 1993
This edition first published 1994
Reprinted 1994, 1995

A CIP catalogue record for this book is available
from the British Library

ISBN 0 19 279831 6 (hardback)
ISBN 0 19 272284 0 (paperback)

Typeset by Oxford Publishing Services, Oxford
Printed in Hong Kong

for Jonathan Gili

Contents

S UPPOSE we first gallop to Banbury Cross,
To visit that lady upon a white horse,
And see if it's true that her fingers and toes
Make beautiful music, wherever she goes.

Knee-Jogging Rhymes

These are very rhythmic rhymes where the baby rides on your knees or crossed legs. The rate of jogging varies with the rhythm of the words, but usually starts quite gently and ends vigorously.

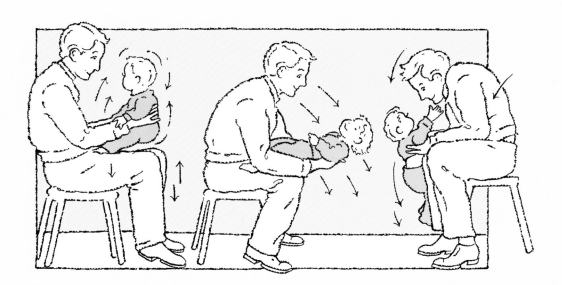

Ride a cock-horse

Ride a cock-horse to Banbury Cross,
To see a fine lady upon a white horse;
With rings on her fingers and bells on her toes,
She shall have music wherever she goes.

Ride a cock-horse to Banbury Cross,
To see what poor Tommy can buy,
A penny white loaf, a penny white cake,
And a twopenny apple pie.

Ride away

Ride away, ride away,
Johnny shall ride,

And he shall have pussy cat tied to one side,
(slip child to one side)
And he shall have puppy dog tied to the other,
(slip child to other side)
And Johnny shall ride to see his grandmother.

One to make ready

One to make ready,
Two to prepare,
Good luck to the tortoise,
And away goes the hare!

Trot, trot, trot

Trot, trot, trot,
Go and never stop.
Trudge along, my little pony,
Where 'tis rough and where 'tis stony.
Go and never stop,
Trot, trot, trot, trot, TROT!

Here comes a lady

Here comes a lady with her little baby,
    A nim, a nim, a nim.

Here comes my lord with his trusty sword,
    A trot, a trot, a trot.

Here comes old Jack with a broken pack,
    A gallop, a gallop, a gallop.

A farmer went trotting

A farmer went trotting
    Upon his grey mare,
      Bumpety, bumpety, bump!
With his daughter behind him
    So rosy and fair,
      Lumpety, lumpety, lump!

A raven cried 'Croak'
    And they all tumbled DOWN,
    (*slip child down between knees*)
      Bumpety, bumpety, bump!
The mare broke her knees,
    And the farmer his crown,
      Lumpety, lumpety, lump!

The mischievous raven
    Flew laughing away,
      Bumpety, bumpety, bump!
And he vowed he would serve them
    The same the next day,
      Lumpety, lumpety, lump!

This is the way the ladies ride

This is the way the ladies ride,
Trippetty tee!
Trippetty tee!
This is the way the ladies ride,
Trippetty, tripetty tee!

This is the way the gentlemen ride,
Gallopy–gallop!
Gallopy–gallop!
This is the way the gentlemen ride,
Gallopy–gallopy–gallop!

This is the way the farmers ride,
Hobbledy–hoy!
Hobbledy–hoy!
This is the way the farmers ride,
Hobbledy–hoy,
Hobbledy–hoy!
And D–O–W–N into the ditch.

Father and Mother, and Uncle John

Father and Mother, and Uncle John
Went to market,
One by one.
Father fell off!   (*slip child to one side*)
Mother fell off!   (*slip child to other side*)
But Uncle John went on, and on,
And on, and on, and on!

To market, to market

To market, to market,
To buy a fat pig;
Home again, home again,
Jiggety–jig.

To market, to market,
To buy a plum bun,
Home again, home again,
Market is done.

To market, to market,
To buy a fat hog;
Home again, home again,
Jiggety–jog.

Rocking-horse

Now rocking-horse, rocking-horse, where shall we go?
The World's such a very big place you must know.
To see all its wonders, the wise people say,
'Twould take us together a year and a day.

Bouncing and Dancing Rhymes

These are played by bouncing the baby on your lap or holding it while it 'dances' on your knee. Lifting the baby in the air and bringing it down between your knees is a feature of some of the rhymes.

Dance, little baby

Dance, little baby,
Dance up high,
Never mind, baby,
Mother is nigh.

Crow and caper,
Caper and crow,
There little baby
There you go!

Up to the ceiling,
Down to the ground,
Backwards and forwards,
Round and round.

Dance, little baby,
Dance up high,
Never mind, baby,
Mother is nigh.

Katie Beardie

Katie Beardie had a cow,
Black and white about the mou,
Wasn'a that a dainty cow?
     Dance, Katie Beardie!

Katie Beardie had a hen,
Cackled but and cackled ben,
Wasn'a that a dainty hen?
     Dance, Katie Beardie!

Katie Beardie had a cock,
That could spin, and bake, and rock,
Wasn'a that a dainty cock?
     Dance, Katie Beardie!

Katie Beardie had a grice,
It could skate upon the ice,
Wasn'a that a dainty grice?
     Dance, Katie Beardie!

Dance to your daddy

Dance to your daddy,
    My bonnie laddy,
Dance to your daddy,
    My bonnie lamb.

You shall get a fishy,
    In a little dishy,
You shall get a fishy,
    When the boat comes in.

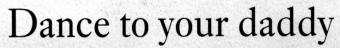

You shall get a coatie,
    And a pair of breekies,
And you'll get an eggy,
    And a bit of ham.

You shall get a pony,
    Fit to ride for ony,
And you'll get a whippy,
    For to make him gang.

Dance to your daddy,
    My bonnie laddy,
Dance to your daddy,
    My bonnie lamb.

Down at the Station

Down at the Station,
Early in the morning,
Two little puffer trains,
All in a row.

Man at the engine,
Turns a little handle,
Chuff–chuff–chuff and away we go,
Chuff–chuff–chuff,
Chuff–chuff–chuff,
Chuff–chuff–chuff–CHUFF.

Higgledy-Piggledy

Higgledy-Piggledy,
My black hen,
She lays eggs
     for gentlemen;
Sometimes nine,
And sometimes ten,
Higgledy-Piggledy,
     my black hen!

Rub–a–dub–dub

Rub–a–dub–dub,
Three men in a tub,
And who do you think were there?
The butcher, the baker,
The candlestick-maker;
All going to the fair.

Cock–crow

The Cock's on the house-top
Blowing his horn.
The bull's in the barn
A–threshing of corn.
The maids in the meadow
Are making the hay.
The ducks in the river
Are swimming away.

Handy-Spandy

Handy-Spandy, jack–a–dandy,
Loved plum cake and sugar candy!
He bought some at a grocer's shop,
And then he goes hop, hop a–hop!

Barber, barber

Barber, barber, shave a pig,
How many hairs will make a wig?
Four and twenty, that's enough,
Give the barber a pinch of snuff.

Patting and Clapping Rhymes

Babies love having their feet patted and their hands clapped. Pat and clap to the rhythm of the words, wiggle legs and tickle as appropriate.

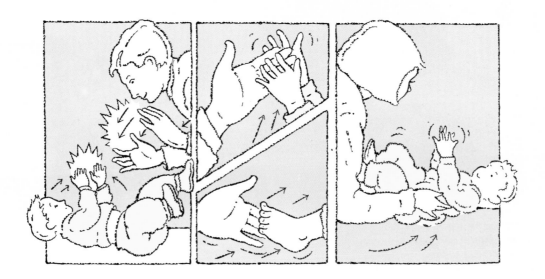

Clap, clap, handies

Clap, clap, handies,
Mummy's wee bairn,
Clap, clap, handies.
Daddy's coming home,
Home to his bonnie wee lassie,
Clap, clap, handies.

Diddle, diddle, dumpling

Diddle, diddle, dumpling,
My son John
Went to bed with his trousers on;
One shoe off and one shoe on,
Diddle, diddle, dumpling,
My son John.

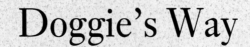

Doggie's Way

Leg over leg   (*cross baby's legs one over the other*)
As the dog went to Dover,
When he came to a stile –
JUMP!
He went over.   (*lift baby on 'jump!'*)

Up to the heavens

Up to the heavens,
Down to the sea,
How many fishes can you see?
One–two–three–four–FIVE.

See-saw Sacradown

See-saw, Sacradown,
Which is the way
To London Town?
One foot up,
The other foot down,
That is the way
To London Town.

The little duck

I think it was the best of luck,
That I was born a little duck,
With yellow feet and yellow shoes,
Just fit to waddle where I choose.

Hob, shoe, hob

Hob, shoe, hob,
(*pat baby's feet*)
Hob, shoe, hob.
Here a nail,
There a nail,
And that's well shod.

Three little ghosties'es

Three little ghosties'es,
Sat on three posties'es,
Eating buttered toasties'es,
Greasing their fisties'es
Up to their wristies'es
Weren't they beasties'es!

Shoe a little horse

Shoe a little horse,
Shoe a little mare,
But let the little colt,
Go bare, bare, bare.

Lullabies and Rocking Rhymes

These are sleeping songs for you and the baby, having a cuddle or gently rocking to and fro or side to side.

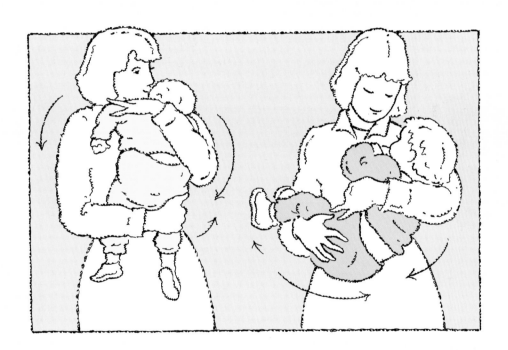

Bye baby bunting

Bye baby bunting,
Daddy's gone a'hunting,
Mummy's gone a'milking,
Sister's gone a'silking,
Brother's gone to buy a skin
To wrap the baby bunting in.

Sleepy Song

Hush–a–bye, baby,
Pussy's a lady,
Mousie has gone to the mill;
And if you don't cry,
She'll come back by and by,
So hush–a–bye, baby, lie still.

Lullaby

Hush–a–bye, baby
Daddy's away,
Brother and sisters
Have gone out to play;
But here by your cradle,
Dear baby, I'll keep,
To guard you from danger,
And sing you to sleep.

Baby Beds

Little lambs, little lambs,
Where do you sleep?
'In the green meadow
With mother sheep.'

Little birds, little birds,
Where do you rest?
'Close to our mother
In a warm nest.'

Baby dear, baby dear,
Where do you lie?
'In my warm bed
With mother close by.'

Evening

Hush, hush, little baby,
The sun's in the west;
The lamb in the meadow
Has lain down to rest.

The bough rocks the bird now,
The flower rocks the bee,
The wave rocks the lily,
The wind rocks the tree.

And I rock the baby
So softly to sleep,
She must not awaken
Till daisy-buds peep.

Rock–a–bye baby

Rock–a–bye baby on the tree top,
When the wind blows the cradle will rock;
When the bough breaks the cradle will fall,
Down will come baby, cradle and all.